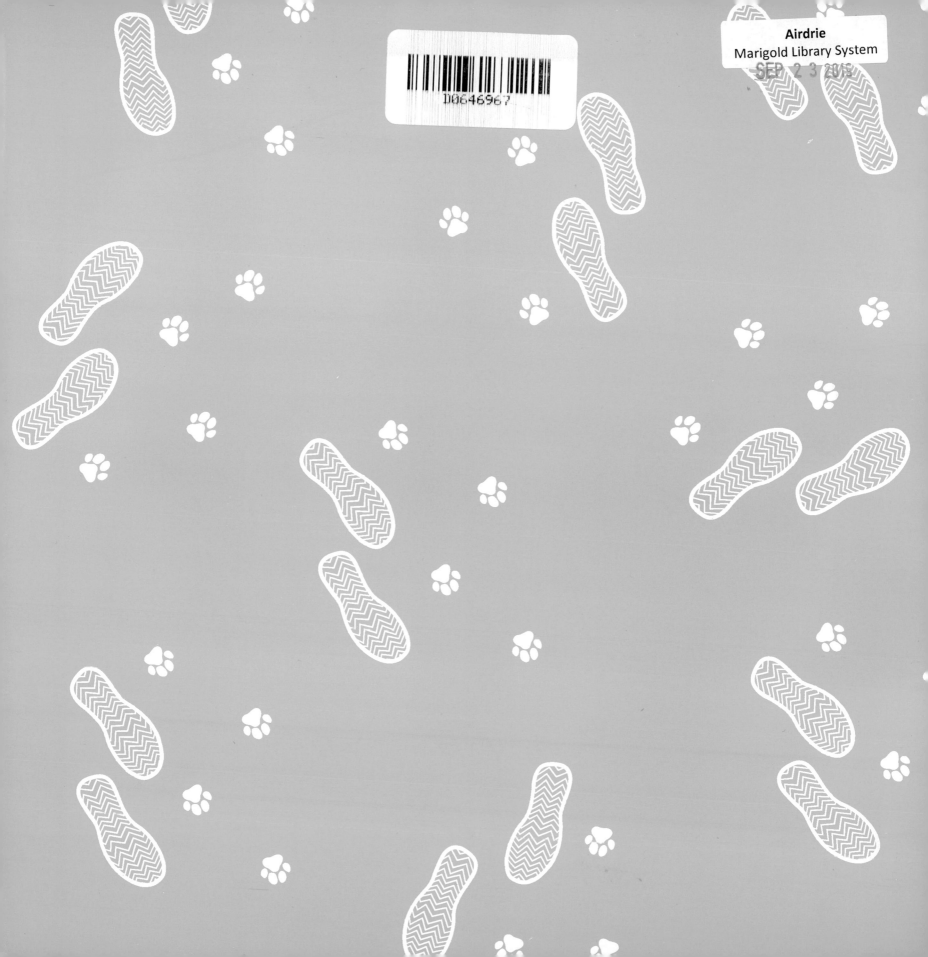

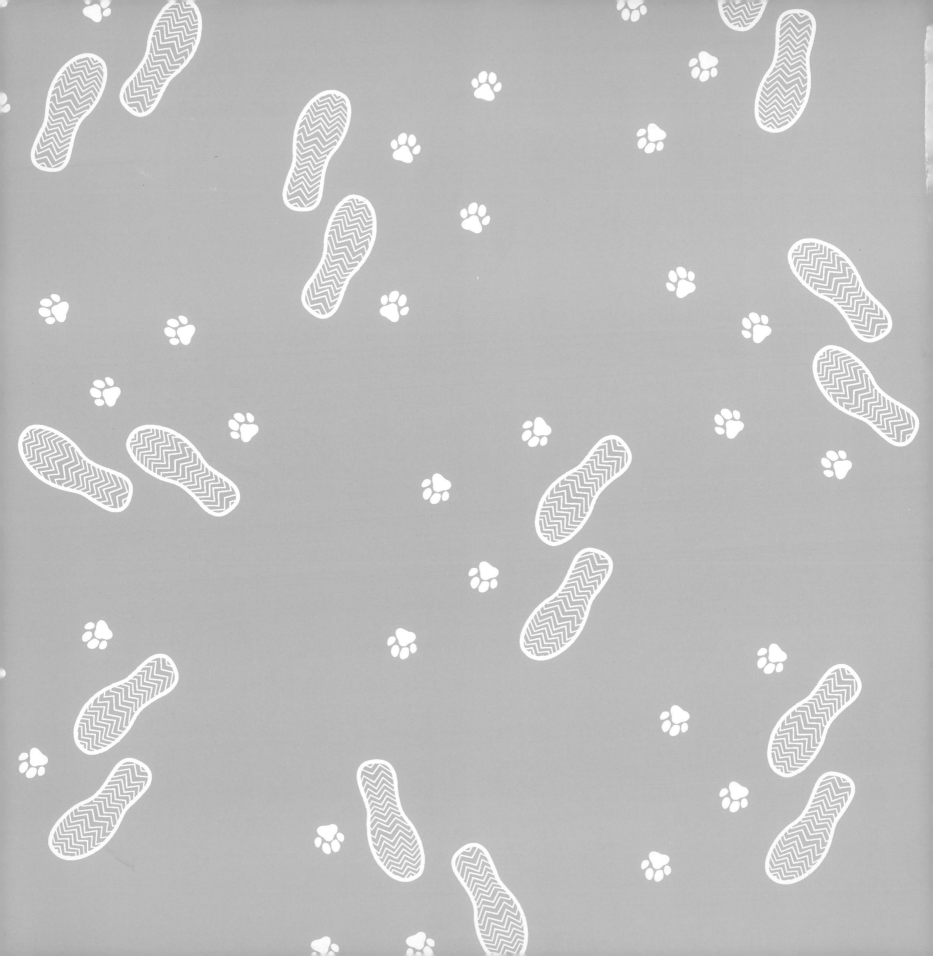

Two Brothers, One Tail

Words by **Richard T. Morris** • Pictures by **Jay Fleck**

PHILOMEL BOOKS

Philomel Books
an imprint of Penguin Random House LLC
375 Hudson Street
New York, NY 10014

Text copyright © 2019 by Richard T. Morris.
Illustrations copyright © 2019 by Jay Fleck.

Philomel Books is a registered trademark of Penguin Random House LLC.
Library of Congress Cataloging-in-Publication Data is available upon request.
Manufactured in China
ISBN 9781524740856
10 9 8 7 6 5 4 3 2 1

Edited by Jill Santopolo.
Design by Ellice M. Lee.
Text set in Clarendon.

The art was done in pencil with color and texture added digitally.

For Clay
—RM

To Pepper, Lily, and Otis
—JF

Two brothers one tail

A tale of two brothers

See for yourself

They're just like each other

Two brothers two hands
Two brothers four paws

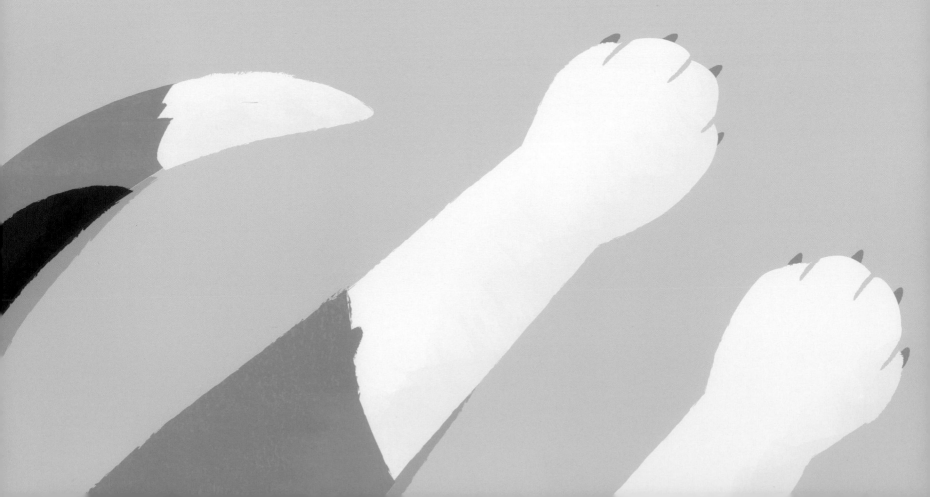

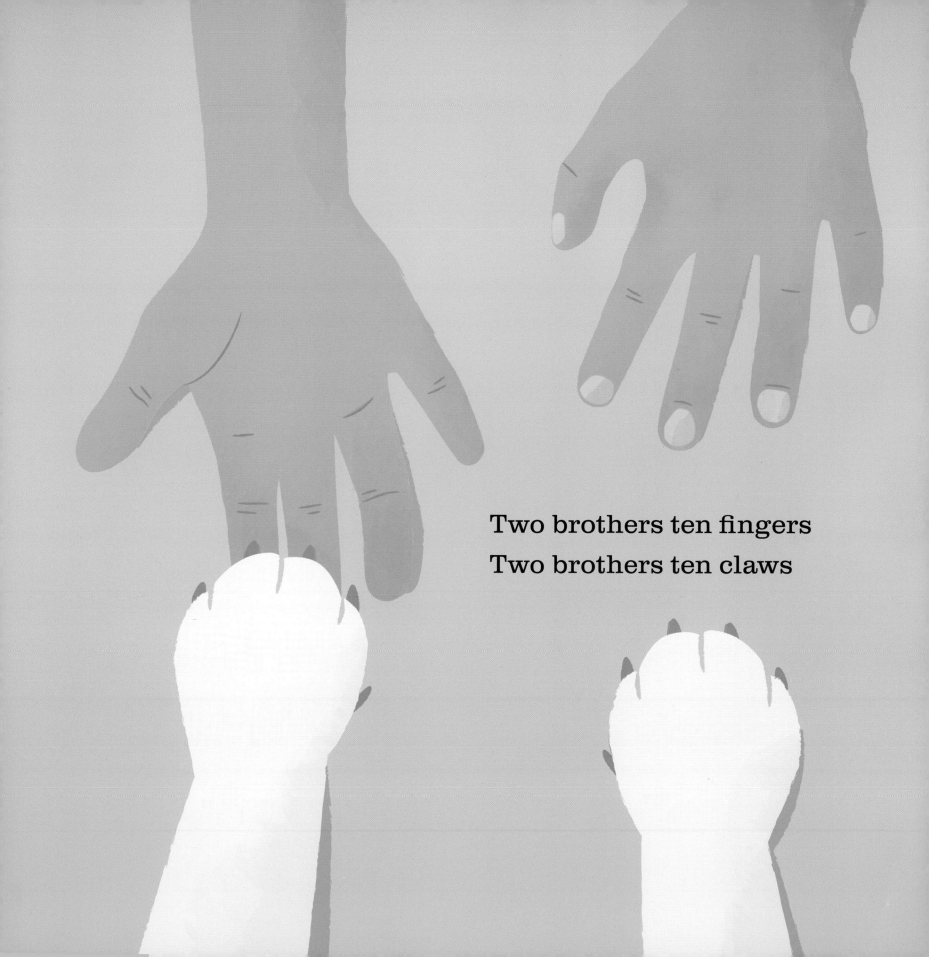

Two brothers ten fingers
Two brothers ten claws

Two brothers four ears
Two brothers six legs

Two brothers four eyes
Two brothers one begs

Two brothers they sing
Two brothers one croons

Two brothers one howls
Two brothers in tune

Two brothers one coat
Two brothers with hair

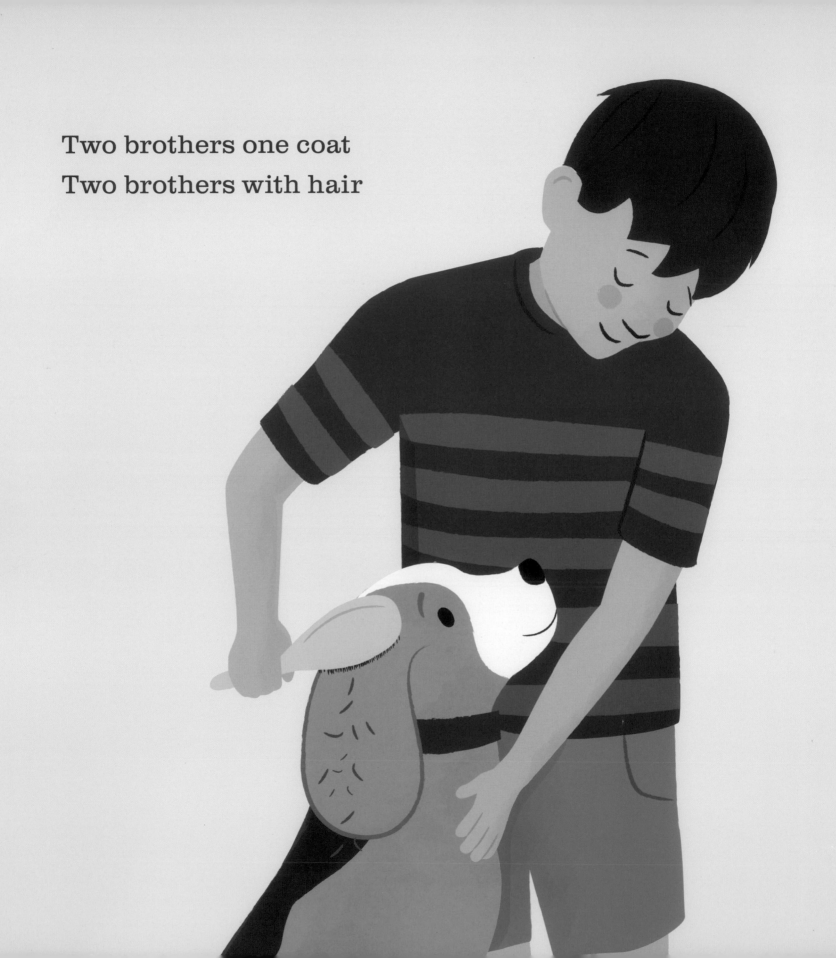

Two brothers one sheds
Two brothers who cares!

Two brothers one car
Two brothers pick spots

Two brothers one belted
Two brothers one not

Two brothers outside

Two brothers run, play

Two brothers inseparable

Two brothers all day

Two brothers two bowls

Two brothers no less

Two brothers they dine

Two brothers . . .

. . . big mess!

Two brothers one muzzle

Two brothers two heads
Two brothers twenty whiskers

Two brothers one bed

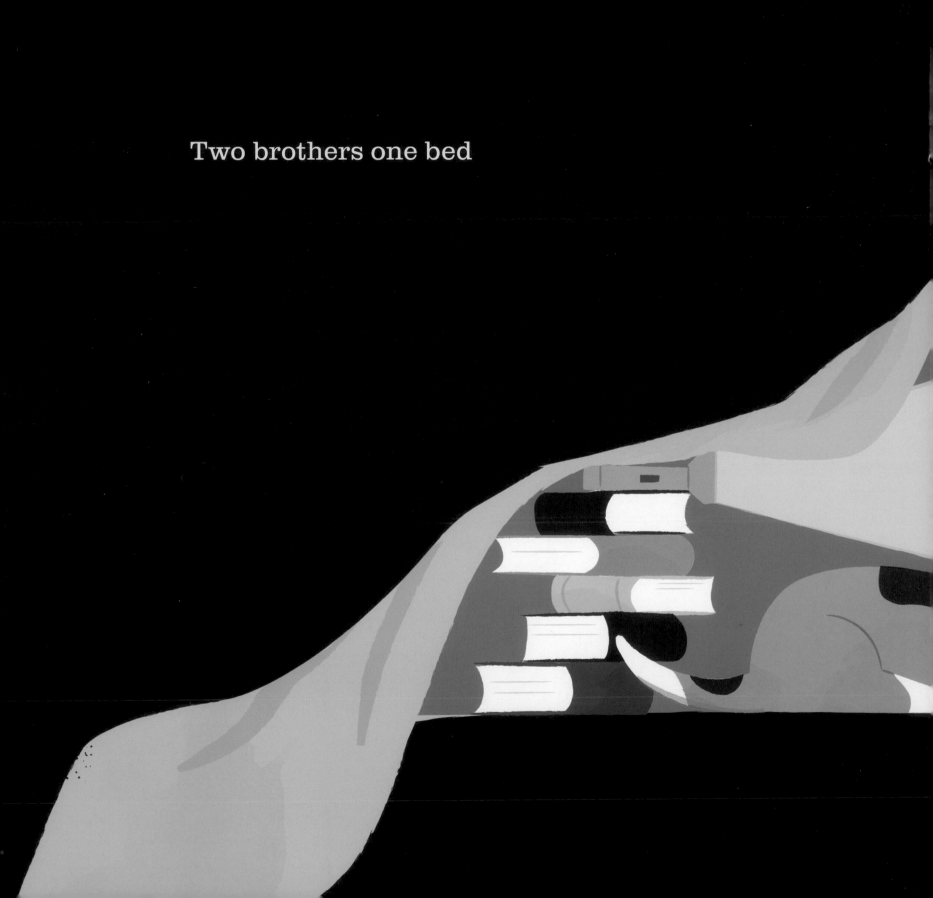

Two brothers one tail
A tale of two brothers
A boy and his dog
A love like no other

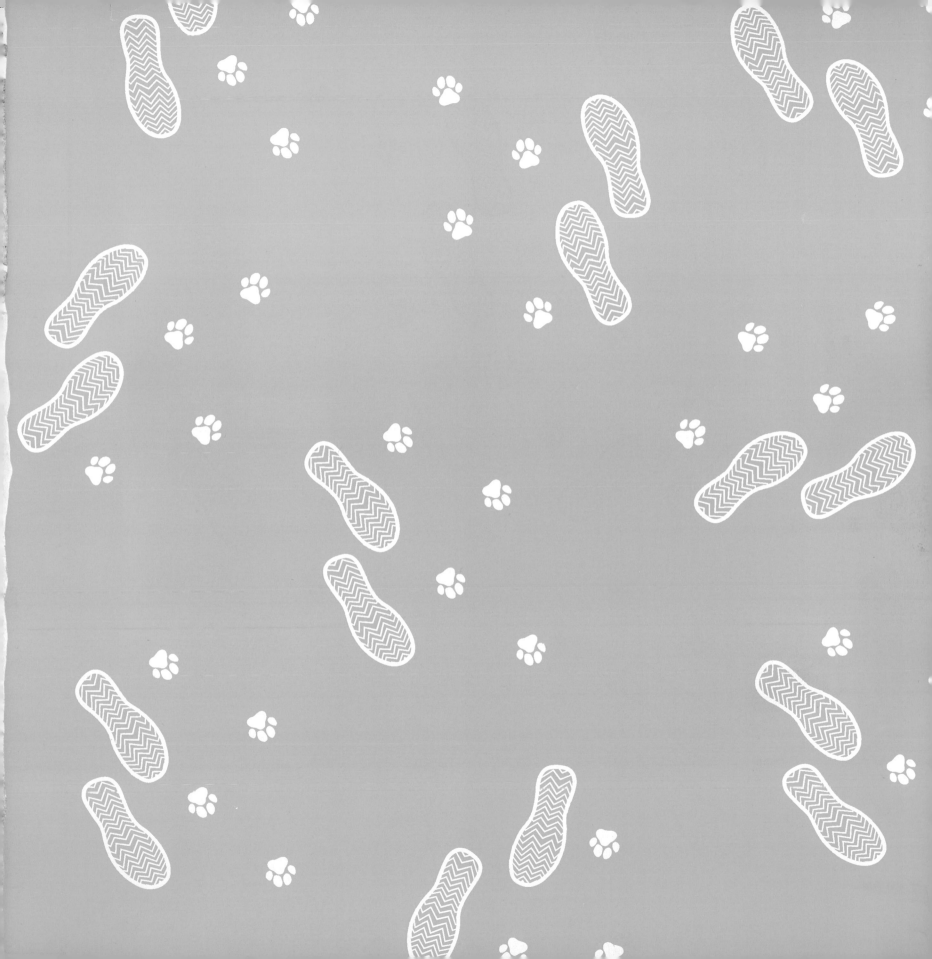

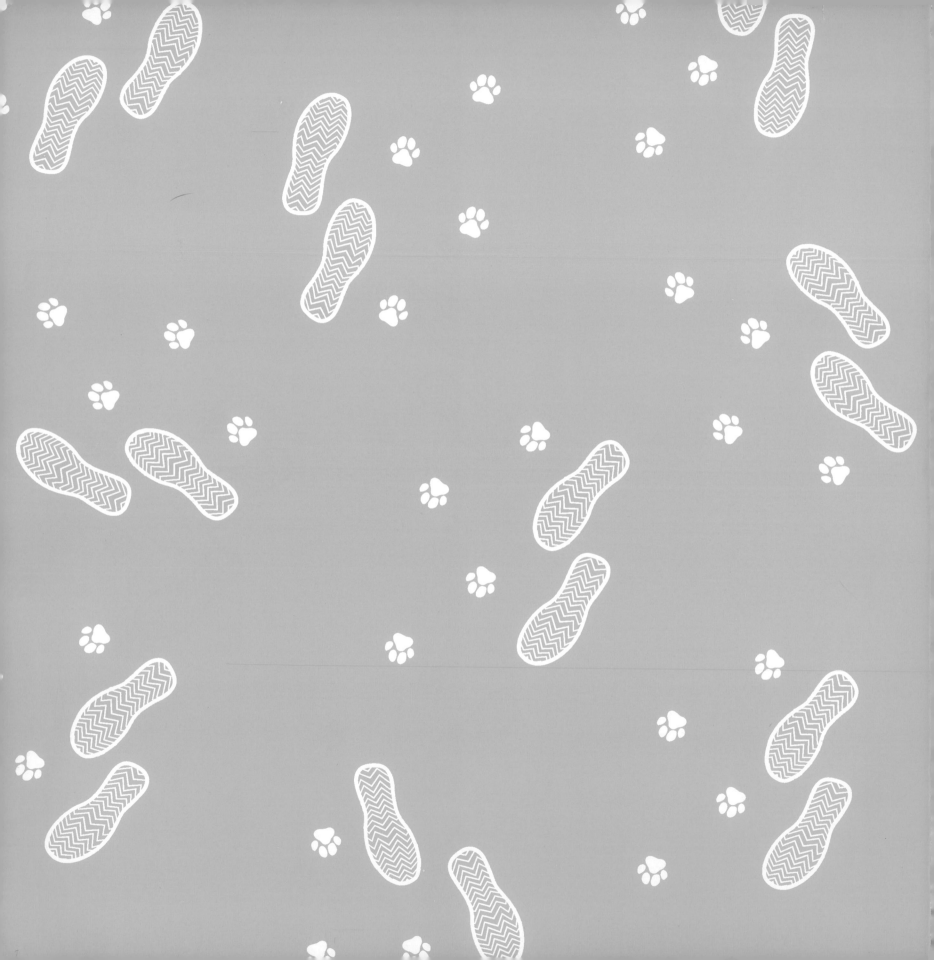